W9-BMT-724

THE INVISIBLE MOOSE

DENNIS HASELEY

ILLUSTRATED BY **STEVEN KELLOGG**

 Dial Books for Young Readers

For Connor and Claudia —D.H.

To the great Wally with love —S.K.

DIAL BOOKS FOR YOUNG READERS • A division of Penguin Young Readers Group • Published by The Penguin Group • Penguin Group (USA) Inc., 375 Hudson Street, New York, NY 10014, U.S.A. • Penguin Group (Canada), 90 Eglinton Avenue East, Suite 700, Toronto, Ontario, Canada M4P 2Y3 (a division of Pearson Penguin Canada Inc.) • Penguin Books Ltd, 80 Strand, London WC2R 0RL, England • Penguin Ireland, 25 St. Stephen's Green, Dublin 2, Ireland (a division of Penguin Books Ltd) • Penguin Group (Australia), 250 Camberwell Road, Camberwell, Victoria 3124, Australia (a division of Pearson Australia Group Pty Ltd) • Penguin Books India Pvt Ltd, 11 Community Centre, Panchsheel Park, New Delhi - 110 017, India • Penguin Group (NZ), Cnr Airborne and Rosedale Roads, Albany, Auckland 1310, New Zealand (a division of Pearson New Zealand Ltd) • Penguin Books (South Africa) (Pty) Ltd, 24 Sturdee Avenue, Rosebank, Johannesburg 2196, South Africa • Penguin Books Ltd, Registered Offices: 80 Strand, London WC2R 0RL, England • Text copyright © 2006 by Dennis Haseley • Illustrations copyright © 2006 by Steven Kellogg • All rights reserved. • Designed by Lily Malcom • Text set in Hiroshige Book • Manufactured in China on acid-free paper • 10 9 8 7 6 5 4 3 2 1

Library of Congress Cataloging-in-Publication Data
Haseley, Dennis.
  The invisible moose / Dennis Haseley ; illustrated by Steven Kellogg.
      p. cm.
  Summary: When his beloved is captured by Steel McSteal, a shy moose summons his courage and, with the help of an invisibility potion, sets off to rescue her in New York City.
  ISBN 0-8037-2892-1
  [1. Moose—Fiction. 2. New York (N.Y.)—Fiction. 3. Humorous stories.] I. Kellogg, Steven, ill. II. Title.
  PZ7.H2688In 2006
  [Fic]—dc22   2004023102

The full-color artwork was prepared using ink and pencil line, watercolor washes, and acrylic paints.

She was a beautiful moose, the most beautiful in the forest. He was a shy young moose and he was in love with her. But there were many older, stronger moose who tried to win her hoof. They fought each other in front of her, their antlers smashing noisily. His own antlers had once been struck by a falling tree, and now they twisted upward like twin question marks. So what chance did he have? He didn't think she even knew who he was. To her, he was probably invisible.

And once he had been. Hidden behind trees, he had watched her free a groundhog from a trap. He told himself then that, unlike the other moose, it wasn't just her beauty that he loved. It was also her goodness.

He dreamed of revealing this, of showing her he was different from the others. But for a long time he didn't have the courage to approach her. Until the first day of winter came to the Canadian woods where they lived. On that day he decided he would talk to her at last.

"You want to ask me something?" she said as he walked up to her. It was his twisted horns that made her think so. "Well, in fact I . . ." She looked at him and smiled. A sweet, wonderful smile. He thought he would do anything to be near that smile.

"Nice weather," he said, although in fact it was starting to sleet.

A tremendous ruckus stopped her from answering. Something was approaching through the forest—yapping and crashing and roaring. All of the other moose opened their eyes wide in alarm.

"Sounds like a big moose-quito," he said, trying to be funny and fearless.

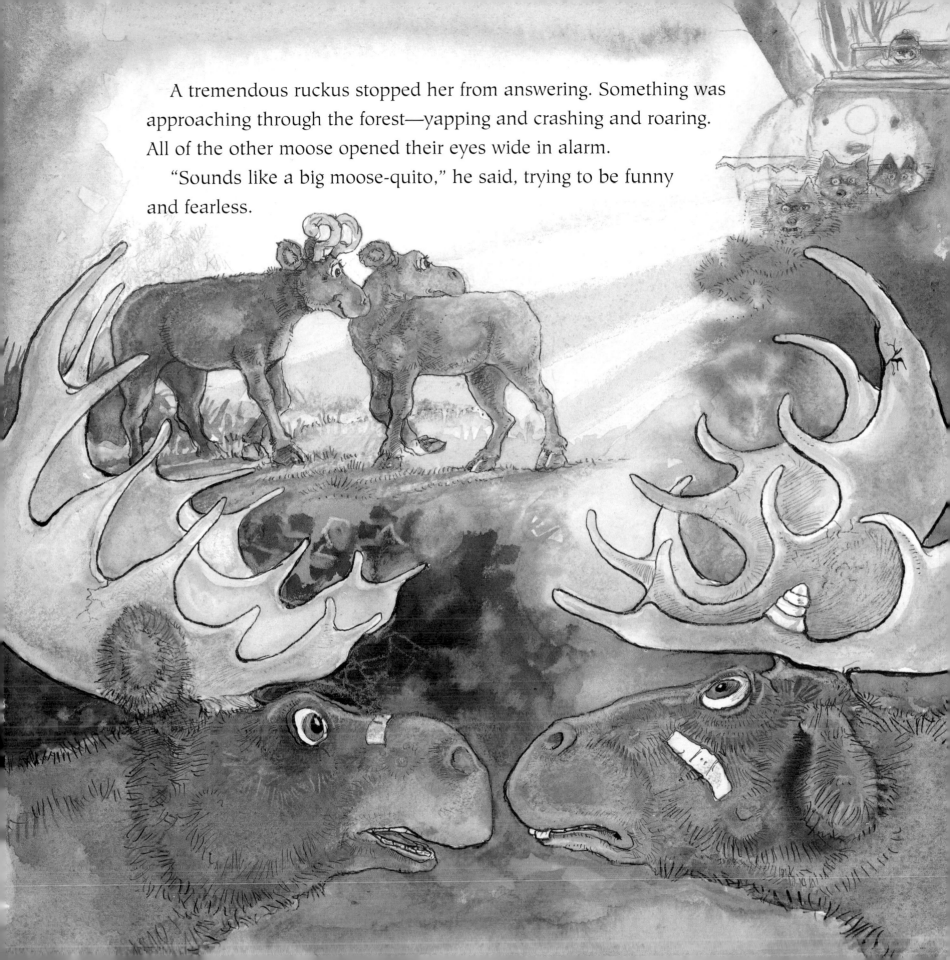

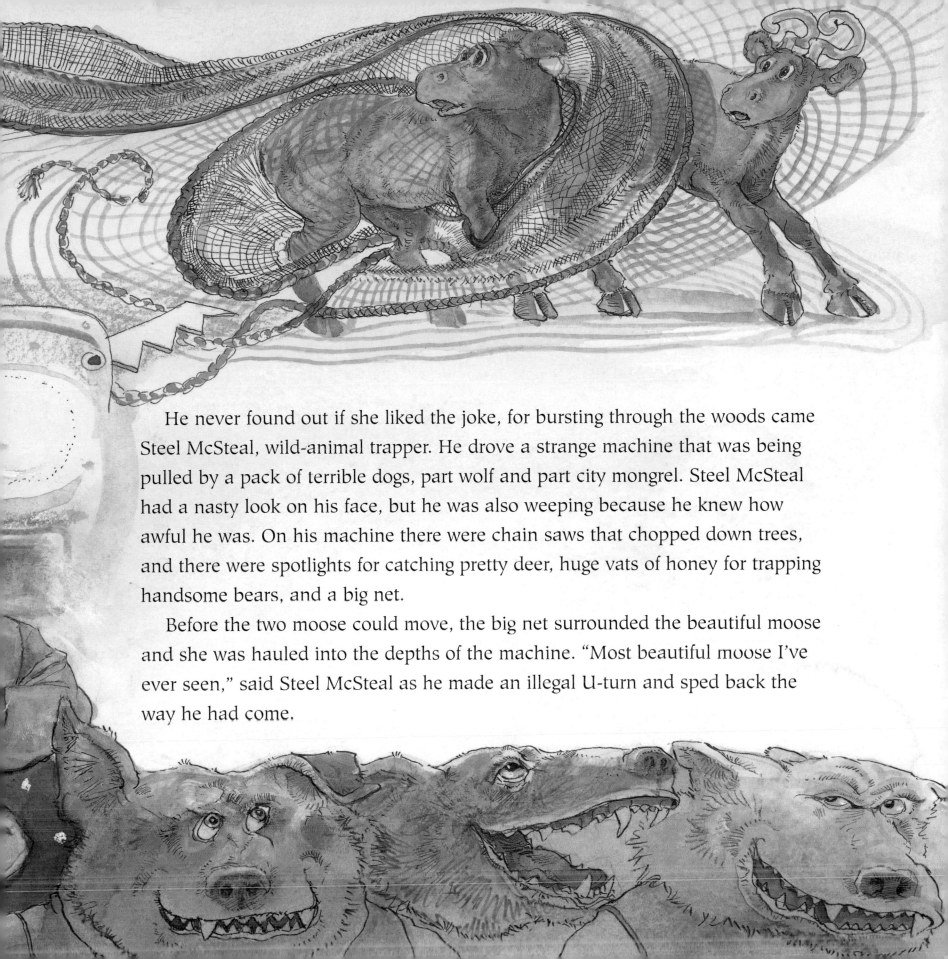

He never found out if she liked the joke, for bursting through the woods came Steel McSteal, wild-animal trapper. He drove a strange machine that was being pulled by a pack of terrible dogs, part wolf and part city mongrel. Steel McSteal had a nasty look on his face, but he was also weeping because he knew how awful he was. On his machine there were chain saws that chopped down trees, and there were spotlights for catching pretty deer, huge vats of honey for trapping handsome bears, and a big net.

Before the two moose could move, the big net surrounded the beautiful moose and she was hauled into the depths of the machine. "Most beautiful moose I've ever seen," said Steel McSteal as he made an illegal U-turn and sped back the way he had come.

All of the tough male moose raced forward to rescue her, and the shy young moose did too. But as they reached a treeless part of the forest, they were met by gunshots. It was hunting season, and the moose knew they were not safe outside the thick trees where they could hide. Giving up, they ran back into the woods. Only the young moose stayed a moment longer, squinting to see the disappearing machine.

"New York City," he said, reading the license plate frame. "I wonder what that means." As he ran back into the forest, he decided to visit Professor Owl McFowl, who was a scientist and geographer. Maybe he would know how to help.

"You want to ask me something?" said Professor McFowl as he mixed up some formulas.

"Well, I—"

"You don't need to. I can see it in your face! It's trouble with a girl!"

The young moose sighed. He remembered her smile. "Professor, what is New York City?"

"A faraway place," said the owl. "I'll show you. Here we are, way up here. And here's the United States border, way down here. And even farther down is New York City."

"Is it a forest?" asked the young moose.

"No," said the owl. "But it's big like a forest."

"And could I go there?"

"There are no moose in New York City," said the owl.

"There's one," said the young moose.

"You could never get there," said the owl. "As soon as you left the forest, you'd be hunted. And even if you made it away safely, you're too big, and you'd be spotted—unless . . ."

"Unless?" said the young moose hopefully.

"There is a formula I've been working on that will turn things invisible."

"Invisible!" said the young moose. "I need that formula!"

"She's that important?"

"Yes," the young moose said, and with hardly a pause he drank down the liquid.

Immediately, he started to disappear. First his
tail, then his hooves, and then up his body until
just his antlers could be seen.

"More questions?" said the owl. But in fact the
shy young moose was too busy noticing how much
of him was missing.

"Where am I?" he wailed.

"You're invisible!" said the owl, a gleam of pride in his eyes as the young moose's antlers disappeared.

Professor McFowl gave him another bottle of the formula in case the effect wore off in an awkward spot. The young moose put the bottle in the hollow part of his hoof.

"I can't thank you enough," he said. "And what do I take when I want to be visible again?"

"Now *that's* a very good question," said the owl.

The next day the young moose set off. He had memorized the directions: "Make a right at Quebec, and follow the water." Dawn was breaking as he left the forest. He trotted past the hunters and began the long journey south.

Standing on logs, he rafted down rivers.

He walked across fields of ice, his breath making smoke in the cold air.

He passed through small towns.

Crossing the border did not pose a problem.

Finally he arrived in New York City!

But the owl was right: There were no moose to be seen. And there were lots of buildings and crowds. He worried that in this strange forest of brick and metal, he would never find the one moose who was there.

He looked for her everywhere.
The lights of Broadway hurt his eyes.
He felt queasy on the Staten Island Ferry.

He liked Central Park, but the carriage horses reared up when he tried
to speak to them.

One night, very hungry, he walked into a fancy restaurant and started grazing where the salads were being made. If people had been watching closely, they would have seen carrots and lettuce and mushrooms disappearing in the air.

When he heard a woman say, "I'll have the mousse," he turned his head suddenly and his invisible antlers knocked into a waiter's tray. Had they cooked his beautiful moose? Was this why he couldn't find her?

Hardly able to look, he lowered his head in despair. But when he did peek, he only saw a waiter bringing the woman a bowl of chocolate pudding. Relief flooded him, and he vowed to find her, no matter what it took.

He followed the scent down an alley, into a street, down another alley. He was about to turn back when a sign on a building caught his eye: MOST BEAUTIFUL MOOSE. ADMISSION $10. Through a lit window he saw her! She was inside a huge cage. Tears had made little rivers in the fur of her nose. In a corner of the room, Steel McSteal was sleeping in a chair, having bad dreams. If he had been awake, he would have seen his door open and then, after a little while, close.

The invisible moose softly walked over to the cage.

"Hello," he said gently.

"Now I'm hearing voices," cried the beautiful moose.

"No, you're not," said the invisible moose. "It is I."

"If there's someone there, then you're so small that I can't see you.
Strange, though: You sound and smell, not like a mouse, but a moose."

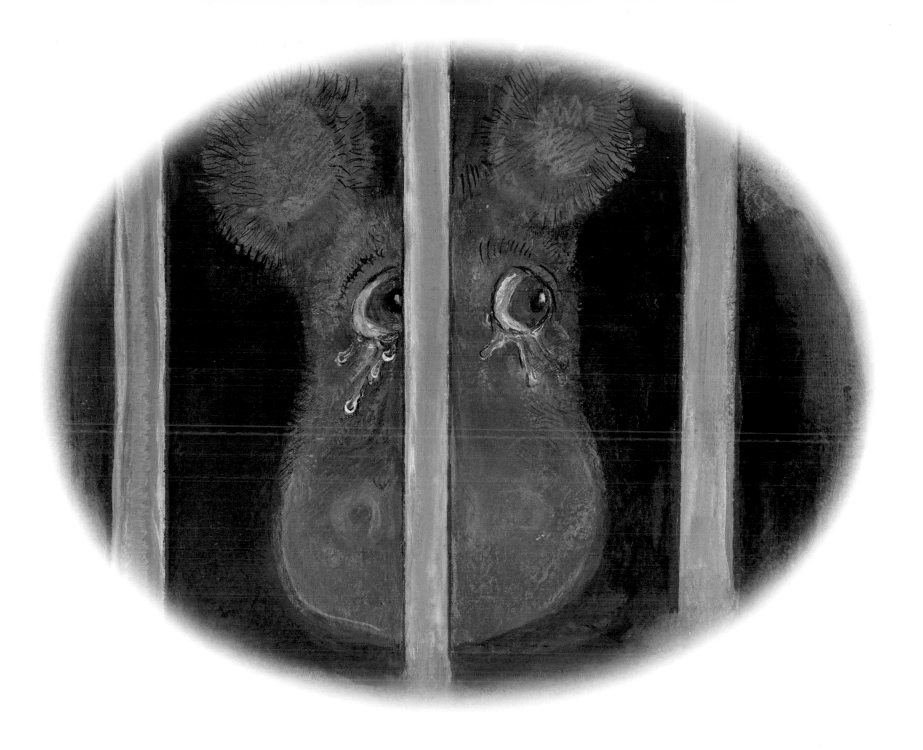

"Thank you," said the invisible moose, who suddenly felt embarrassed.
He hardly knew her, and yet he'd traveled miles from home and was now
doing a terrible job of re-introducing himself.

"Where are you?" the beautiful moose said nervously.

"Just a moment," said the invisible moose. "I'll show you." From around the room he found gloves, shoes, sunglasses, a roll of bandages, and a large robe. "Close your eyes," he said. Then the invisible moose wound the bandages around his head and antlers and put on the clothing. "Now you can look," he said. "Don't be frightened."

She stared at him a moment, her eyes wide. "You're a very unusual moose," she said. "And is there something you want to ask me?"

"No," he answered. "Under these bandages and clothes, I'm a regular moose. I'm the same moose you were talking to when you were stolen. Except now I'm invisible."

"I remember you," she said, and gave him the smile that he knew so well.

"I've come to rescue you," he said. And then, suddenly shy again: "Shall we go?"

"I'd love to be rescued by you," said the beautiful moose. "But I'm locked in this cage. And even if I could get out, they'd see me on the streets." More tears ran down her nose.

"Unless . . ." she said. "Unless I was invisible too."

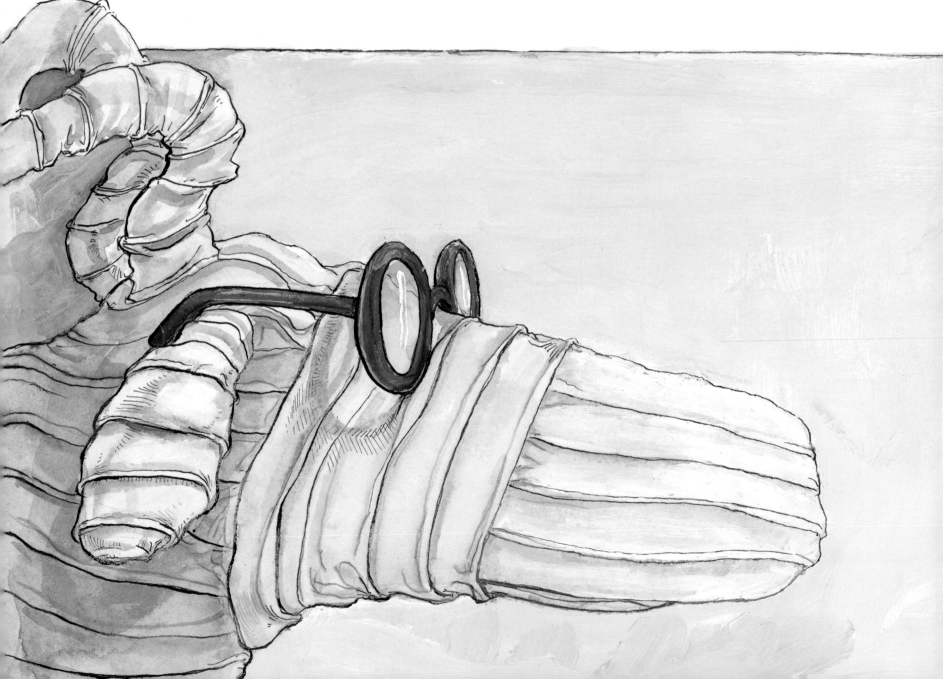

"But you're too beautiful to turn invisible," he blurted out.

"Do you like me just because I'm beautiful?" she asked, smiling at him through her tears.

He felt the warmth of her smile. "No," he said, and as he said it, he knew it was true. "I love you for your heart."

"Well, you can't see my heart," she said. "Just like I can't see your courage. But I know it's there."

He stared at her another moment. Then slowly, a bit sadly, he lifted his hoof, pulled off the glove, and removed the bottle of formula. "Drink this," he said.

She quickly began to disappear. First her tail, then her hooves, and then up her body, until only her smile was left. Then it, too, disappeared, and he felt a catch in his throat.

In the corner of the room, Steel McSteal snorted in his sleep, and the costumed moose quickly took off his clothes and bandages. He rather liked the way the sunglasses looked, but he removed those as well, just as Steel McSteal woke up. The trapper rubbed the sleep from his eyes, glanced toward the cage—and then jumped to his feet.

"Robbers!" he cried. He unlocked the cage, rushed in, and the beautiful moose simply walked out.

"It still smells like moose in this room," muttered Steel McSteal. "In fact, it smells twice as strong!"

Suddenly, the cage door shut and bolted. Steel McSteal watched through the bars as the door to the street opened, stayed that way awhile, and then politely closed itself again. The trapper stamped his feet and then he started to cry.

Outside, it was starting to snow. The two invisible moose ran through the streets and over a bridge, feeling happy and free. Soon they were beyond the city.

They looked back at it a moment.

"I'll miss the food," he said, and laughed. In the sky, they could see stars peeking through.

"I remember the way back," he said. "And then, if we want, I'm sure Professor McFowl will come up with another formula to make us visible again."

"If we want," she said.

He looked over to where he knew she was standing.

"I feel you're smiling at me now," he said.

"I am," she said. They stood a moment next to each other, feeling warm in the snow. "Now, shall we go?"

"Yes," he said.

On the fresh white ground, their tracks appeared,
two by two, as they headed north, and home.